HARRIET AND THE ROLLER COASTER

tickets for Roller Coaster

10¢

HARRIET AND THE ROLLER COASTER

NANCY CARLSON

Carolrhoda Books, Inc. / Minneapolis

This book is available in two editions:
Library binding by Carolrhoda Books, Inc., a division of Lerner Publishing Group
Soft cover by First Avenue Editions, an imprint of Lerner Publishing Group
241 First Avenue North
Minneapolis, MN 55401 U.S.A.

Website address: www.lernerbooks.com

Library of Congress Cataloging-in-Publication Data

Carlson, Nancy L.
    Harriet and the roller coaster / by Nancy Carlson
        p.   cm.
    Summary: Harriet accepts her friend George's challenge to ride the frightening roller coaster and finds out that she is the brave one.
    ISBN: 1–57505–053–6 (lib. bdg. : alk. paper)
    ISBN: 1–57505–202–4 (pbk. : alk. paper)
    [1. Dogs—Fiction. 2. Rabbits—Fiction. 3. Courage—Fiction.
  4. Roller coasters—Fiction.] I. Title.
PZ7.C21665 Hap 2003
[E]—dc21   2002013922

Manufactured in the United States of America
1 2 3 4 5 6 – JR – 08 07 06 05 04 03

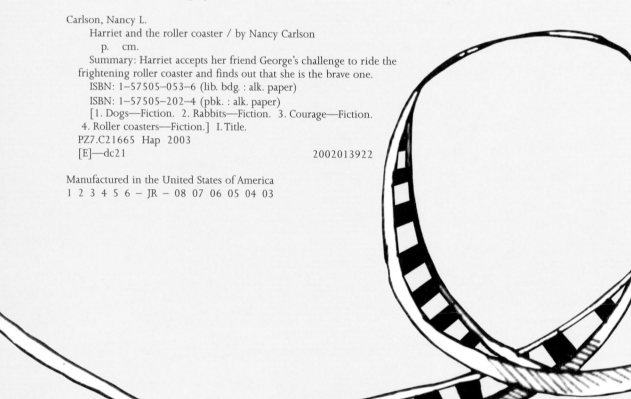

For Jeanne and Mary,
because they take the chances I don't!

On the last day of school, Harriet's whole class
was going to the amusement park. Everyone looked
forward to the day.

"I'm going to ride on the big roller coaster,"
George told Harriet. "It's so big, you can't see the
top. I know. My big sister told me."

"It goes so fast that if you don't hold on, you'll fall right out."

"I bet you're too scared to ride the roller coaster.
You'd probably start crying."

"I am *not* scared," said Harriet. "I'll ride on your old roller coaster. You just wait and see."

That night Harriet didn't sleep very well.

The next morning, when it was time to get on the bus for the amusement park, she felt a little sick.

"See you on the roller coaster," said George. "If you don't chicken out."

As soon as they got to the amusement park, George said, "Come on, Harriet. Let's get our tickets for the roller coaster. Unless you're too scared."

"I am *not* scared," said Harriet.

"Good," said George. "Then hurry up."

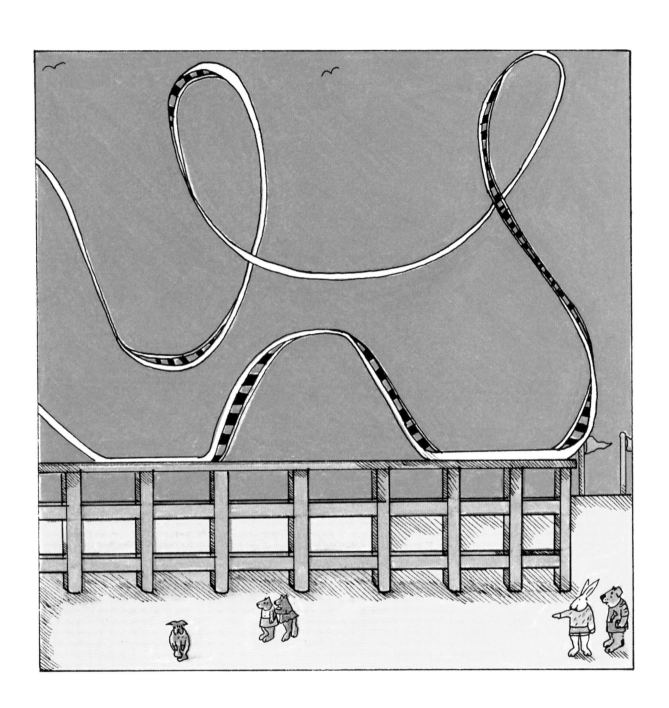

"Oh, boy," said George.

"I can't wait!"

"We're next."

"There's still time for you to chicken out."

"Here we go. Harriet, you're going to be sooooo scared."

The roller coaster went up and up. Harriet had never been so high.

"This is great," said George.

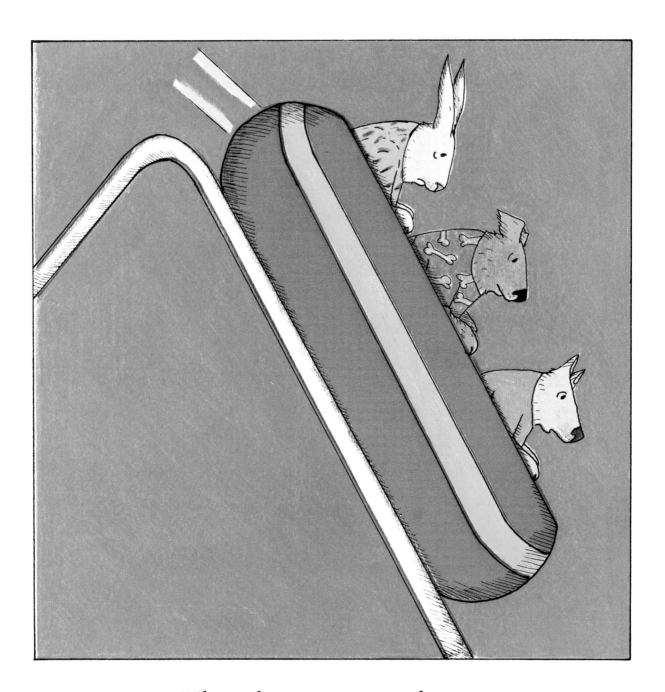

Then they were over the top.

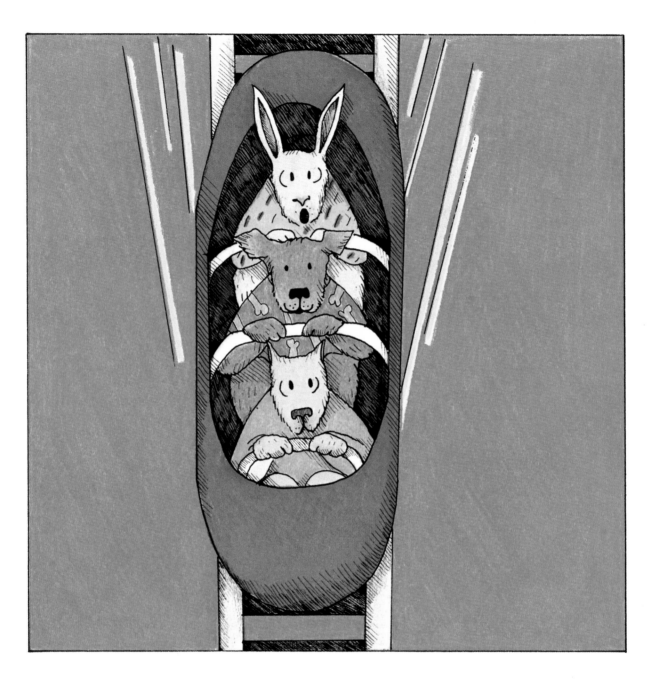

"Hey!" said Harriet. "This isn't so bad."
"Ooof!" said George.

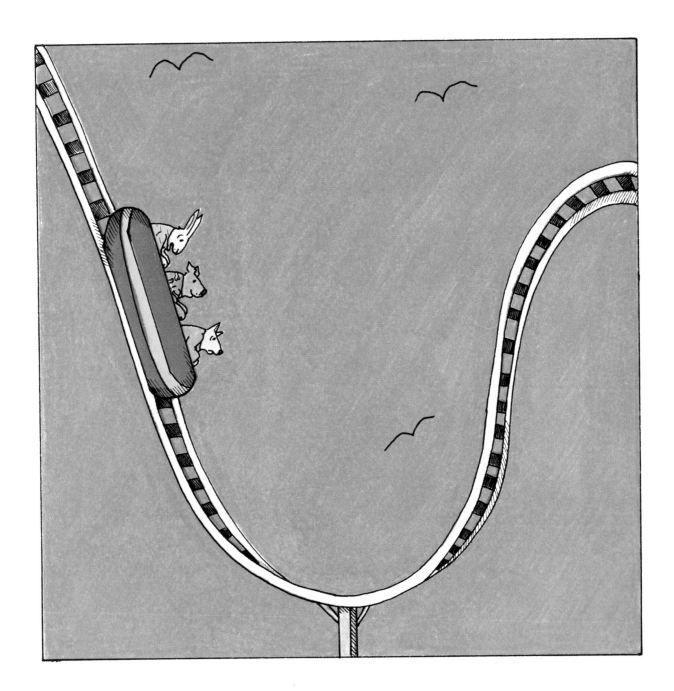

"I like it!" said Harriet.
"Help!" said George.

"Yippee!" yelled Harriet.
"Mommy!" yelled George.

"Is it over already?" said Harriet.

"I'm going again. That was fun!"
"I'd better sit down," said George.

So Harriet rode the roller coaster all day long . . .

. . . while George sat quietly on a bench.